Darwin

Dragonboy

Drako

To my son, Marcus, the original Dragonboy. Because of your inspiration, beautiful sense of wonder, and unique imagination, Dragonboy and Drako now truly exist.

About This Book

The illustrations for this book were done in acrylic paints on wood panels. This book was edited by Deirdre Jones and designed by Véronique Lefèvre Sweet. The production was supervised by Nyamekye Waliyaya, and the production editor was Annie McDonnell. The text was set in Nicolas Cochin Regular, and the display type is hand-lettered.

DRAGONBOY

MARCUS
Beware
of
DRAGON!

The
Lair

Written and Illustrated by

Fabio Napoleoni

L B

Little, Brown and Company
New York Boston

Once upon a time,
not so very far away,
behind the farthest door down the hall,
Dragonboy woke up.

"Rise and shine, everyone."

"It's a great day for exploring."
(Every day is a great day for exploring.)

"It's a great day for discovery."
(Every day is a great day for discovery.)

"Let's see what's waiting for us."

"What are we looking for?" Darwin asked.

"I don't know," Dragonboy replied. "But I know we will find *something*."
(There's always something waiting for you
if your eyes
and your mind
and your heart
are open.)

THAT WAY

THIS WAY

ADVENTURE

"Let's go *that way*," Drako said, bounding into the woods.

So they did.

Simon
plodded.

Dragonboy
ran.

Yellow Kitty
sauntered.

Darwin
ambled.

And Drako
rushed.

Yellow Kitty soon made the first discovery.

"I wonder how long this piece of string is," she said.

"It's as long as the part in the middle, between the beginning and the end," Dragonboy suggested.

Darwin made the next discovery.

"One thousand, nine hundred and ninety-eight," he said quietly.

"That's twenty-six more daisies than yesterday," Dragonboy admired.

"Where's Simon?" Yellow Kitty wondered.

"Remember it takes him twice as long to get half as far," said Dragonboy.

"Let's catch up to him!" Drako roared.

So they did.

Dragonboy
dashed.

Yellow Kitty
pranced.

Darwin
marched.

And Drako
rocketed...

...right into Simon.

Because Simon is a sloth, and sloths move

very

very

s-l-o-w-l-y.

"Moving slowly is the best way to discover
something new," Dragonboy said.

"Or...some...one...new,"
Simon said slowly.

"Hello," said Dragonboy. "Would you like to play with us?"

"No, thank you," said the unicorn, whose name was Karley. (A name is a good discovery: a bunch of sounds that you already know, attached to someone you don't.)

"I'm too sad to play."

Dragonboy knew there were all kinds
of reasons someone could be sad.

Ice cream falling
on the sidewalk.

Being stuck at
home with the flu.

Losing your
favorite ball.

Wanting a green balloon,
not a blue one.

Or no reason at all.

"I'm not magical," Karley said. "And I can't fly. Unicorns are supposed to be good at those things."

Drako nodded. "Sometimes I have so much energy I feel like I might EXPLODE! Even when I'm supposed to sit still."

"Sloths...are...supposed...to... be...great...climbers," Simon added. "But...I...am... afraid...of...heights."

"What are we talking about?" asked Yellow Kitty. "I got distracted. Are cats supposed to get distracted?"

Darwin had wandered into another field of flowers, so Dragonboy spoke for him. "Darwin isn't very scary for a yeti. But he's the best daisy counter in the world."

"And I am a little boy, but most days I'm happiest being a dragon. It makes me feel like I can do anything."

"And you're okay being different than you're supposed to be?" Karley asked.

"We are already who we are *supposed* to be," said Dragonboy. "Especially when we are together."

Later on that night,
  not so very far away,
    behind the farthest door down the hall,
      Dragonboy snuggled into his warm bed.

"Good night, everyone," he said.
"Today was a great day for discovery."
(And finding a new friend is the
very best kind.)

Also later on that night,
    not so very far away,
        behind a different door, down a different hall,
            Karley discovered something, too.

She was exactly who
she was supposed to be.

Yellow Kitty

Karley

Simon